Ghostly
Tales of
Mississippi

Dedication:

To my mother and father who always believed.

And to my wife, Angelica.

You still mean everything.

And finally—to Brett Ortler for the fantastic editing job and Emily Comer Beaumont for not only her amazing editing skills but also for recommending me for this project. Who knew that when we met in elementary school that we'd go on to work on a book together? Crazy.

In some instances, names and locations have been changed at the request of sources.

Content Warning: This book contains several references to suicide and may not be appropriate for all audiences.

Cover design by Travis Bryant and Scott McGrew
Text Design by Karla Linder
Edited by Emily Beaumont

All images copyrighted.
Images used under license from Shutterstock.com:
Front cover and silhouettes: **Alexander_P:** cat; **Morphart Creation:** plant

10 9 8 7 6 5 4 3 2 1
Ghostly Tales of Mississippi
First Edition 2018
Second Edition 2022
Copyright © 2018 and 2022 by Jeff Duke
Published by Adventure Publications
310 Garfield Street South
Cambridge, Minnesota 55008
(800) 678-7006
www.adventurepublications.net
All rights reserved
Printed in the U.S.A.
ISBN 978-1-64755-309-8 (pbk.); eISBN 978-1-64755-310-4

Ghostly Tales of Mississippi

Jeff Duke

Adventure PUBLICATIONS

Table of Contents

Rosehill Cemetery
Brookhaven, Mississippi

Larry sat in his truck for a moment and finished his breakfast, basking in the warm air that was blasting from the old truck's heater. He was not looking forward to being out in that bitterly cold air today. He enjoyed taking care of the cemetery in Brookhaven. He wasn't confined to some stuffy office and constantly having to deal with coworkers or the public in general. With this job, he was mostly on his own. As long as he didn't give his boss something to complain about, he rarely saw him. But, on days like this, Larry wouldn't mind being stuffed into a warm office somewhere.

As he sat and washed the last of his Egg McMuffin down with coffee, he noticed that one of the office lights was on. He was sure he'd turned it off before he left late yesterday afternoon. In fact, he was positive he'd turned it off. The door to the office was still shut and sealed with a padlock and the windows looked intact, so it was doubtful that anyone had broken in. And it's not like there was anything to steal in there anyway. Maybe he'd simply forgotten to turn the light off. He'd noticed that the older he got, the more he forgot the little things.

Thinking nothing more of it, Larry tossed his breakfast wrapper on the floorboard of the truck and stepped out into the chilly morning. He immediately zipped his jacket all the way up and pulled his knit cap down farther so it covered his ears. It was definitely colder than when he'd left the house. He found himself hoping that it would rain. If it did start raining, he could either go back home or hang out around the little space heater in the office. Either option would be better than working outside today.

The early morning fog was still hugging the ground as Larry grabbed some tools from the back of his truck and made his way to the office door. Out on the cemetery grounds, the tips of tombstones peeked out through the low-hanging fog like little bleak mountaintops. Somewhere in the distant darkness, Larry thought he heard the low rumble of thunder.

"Come on, rain," Larry said to himself as he fumbled at the office padlock with numb fingers. With the lock open, Larry stooped to pick up his thermos of coffee from where he'd set it on the ground when something out in the cemetery caught his eye and caused him to stand up straight.

Out among the tombstones and the fog was an old man. From what Larry could see, he was dressed in a neatly pressed suit, which was odd, considering the horrible weather. The old man's hair was slicked back, and he had a large bushy mustache that looked well groomed and cared for. He stood perfectly still between two tombstones and stared silently at the office. If the old man saw Larry, he didn't acknowledge him. He just stood there perfectly still, his face completely emotionless.

"We ain't open yet, sir," Larry called out to the old man. And then he muttered under his breath, "At least wait until the damn sun is up."

If the old man heard Larry, he didn't show it. He continued to stand perfectly still, with his eyes fixed on the office. Larry wondered if maybe he was one of those elderly people you see all the time on the news whose mind isn't what it once was and who had wandered off. Maybe the guy had dementia?

"You . . . you need some help, sir?" Larry yelled as he started walking toward the man. "Hello? Sir, can you hear me?"

As Larry approached, the old man's head turned ever so slightly, as if he'd just noticed the caretaker walking toward him. And then he vanished. He didn't turn and walk away into the fog. He didn't back into the fog. He just slowly faded away until he was gone.

Larry stopped in his tracks and tried to process what he had just seen. He was completely alone in the graveyard now. There was no trace of the old man who had just been standing there. In the distance, there was another lazy, low rumble of thunder, louder and closer than the one before. There was a faint rattling noise that Larry couldn't place until he realized that it was the sound of his wedding ring tapping against his metal thermos; he was shaking.

After a few moments of stunned silence, Larry muttered something about the chances of rain and walked back to the office in the dull gray morning light.

He snapped the padlock back on the front door and got back into his truck. He was the caretaker here at Rosehill Cemetery, and an old cemetery like Rosehill needed a lot of care.

But today, Rosehill would have to take care of itself, he thought, as he started the truck and drove through the fog, down the winding path, and toward home.

John's Bayou Road
Vancleave, Mississippi

After they related the story of their accident to the state trooper, Barry and Kate stared at him, and he, in turn, stared back. The office was quiet, the only noise coming from a squeaky desk fan as it struggled to turn back and forth. The trooper turned his attention to his laptop, typed a few more lines, and then closed it. Reaching into a drawer from his desk, he took out a battered, faded notebook whose cover was worn from both age and use. He thumbed through various yellowed handwritten pages until he found a blank one.

"OK, Mr. and Mrs. Stevens. Let's go over what happened one more time," he said, as he began writing in the notebook.

Barry and Kate turned to look at each other. It had been a long day—a very long day—and neither really wanted to tell the story again. Kate made a face that said "humor him" and Barry shook his head.

"OK. My wife and I were driving up to my sister's for a wedding. The trip was going fine until I heard…"

"Oh my God. Is that…blood?" Kate said, as she pointed toward an upcoming expanse of road.

Barry looked up from his phone where he was trying to find another podcast to listen to and slowed the car as the red, wet patch on the road came closer. The asphalt ahead was streaked with a red liquid that definitely appeared to be blood. The red mass covered the entire road and stretched on for several feet. Deep crimson and bright-red patches on the edges glistened in the sunlight.

"What the…," Barry muttered to himself. Setting his phone down, he eased the car to the shoulder of the road.

"Um, what do you think you're doing?" asked Kate.

"That's a lot of blood. What if someone is hurt? It's too much to be an animal. I mean, I suppose it could've been a deer or a cow, but, with that much blood, it would've been a hell of an impact and there would probably be a wrecked car along with it. My roommate in college crashed into a deer one night. His truck was pretty much totaled and ended up in a ditch. I just want to take a look."

Barry parked the car halfway onto the shoulder and stepped out. Looking both ways to ensure no traffic was coming, he slowly headed toward the thick liquid patch that covered the highway and knelt near the large puddle. It—whatever it was—had to have happened recently. The blood was still fresh. Fresh enough that it was oozing toward the opposite shoulder, thanks to the natural incline of the highway.

"Kate," he called. "Come check this out. Something got hit—and recently. And this is definitely blood. This stuff hasn't even had time to dry."

Kate exited the car and walked to stand beside her crouched husband. The whole time, her eyes never left the crimson swath on the highway. Barry rose as she approached. "Should we call the highway patrol?" she asked.

"Yeah," he replied. "I want to look around first, though. Check the grass and bushes on the other side. Whatever it was that got creamed, looks like it dragged itself off that side of the road."

The blood trailed over to the opposite side of the highway and disappeared into the knee-high grass. Barry took Kate's hand and began walking to the other side while carefully avoiding the ominous red liquid at their feet.

"Do you hear anything, Barry?" Kate asked, as she scanned the tall grass in front of them.

"I thought I heard a moan or something when I got out of the car. I couldn't tell if it was a person or an animal, though."

"No. Do you hear…anything?"

Barry hadn't noticed it before, but it was deathly quiet. No birds chirping, no insects making insect sounds, nothing. There had been a slight humid breeze when Barry got out of the car, and now that was gone as well. The tall grass in front of them stood completely still. And whatever was out there in the grass was silent and still as well.

"Go ahead and call the highway patrol. Best to let them look at this," Barry said. "I don't like it at all."

"Barry, I'm not getting a signal." Kate replied, as she stared at the screen of her phone.

"What do you mean you're not getting a signal? You were just on the phone with your sister a few minutes ago before we stopped."

"I mean I'm not getting a signal. Nothing."

"Let me take a look," Barry said. "I think you should always be able to call emergency services. They broadcast a special frequency or something just for stuff like 911."

Thinking back on the events that followed, Barry tried to remember if he'd seen the black van coming. He'd try to convince himself that maybe he just hadn't noticed it. Black vans just don't appear out of nowhere. Maybe it had approached them while they were looking for whatever was dead or dying in the grass. But the answer was always "no." One minute the black van wasn't there and the next, it was.

The van's engine roared as it headed straight toward their parked car. The shirtless figure behind the wheel was pale with a scraggly mess of black curly hair that obscured his face as he leaned forward, gripping the wheel and bracing for the impact. Barry grabbed his wife's hand and yanked her toward him as the van slammed into their car in an explosion of glass, plastic, and metal. The force of the collision shot their car down the embankment and it rolled on its side. The driver of the van hadn't used the brakes at all. If anything, he'd sped up. And now the driver, as well as the van, was gone. Barry and Kate were alone on the side of the road. There was no van, no blood. Just them and their demolished car.

"And that's exactly what happened," Barry said, as the trooper jotted in the battered notebook he'd pulled out. "I know it doesn't make any sense, and I don't blame you for not believing us."

The trooper stopped writing and looked up at the couple.

"Oh, I believe you," the trooper replied, as he stared at the notes he'd just written. "You folks aren't the first people this has happened to."

"What do you mean?" asked Kate.

"This notebook belonged to my daddy. He was a state trooper in Vancleave just like me. He started this notebook back in 1973, right after some folks much like yourselves told him pretty much the exact same story. Couple stopped to investigate a bunch of blood on the road and then a black van plowed into their car, only to immediately vanish. Driver of the van is always the same. Some shirtless, scraggly headed guy."

"You're kidding," said Barry.

"Wish I was," the trooper said, as he held up the notebook and thumbed through the pages. The notebook's yellowed pages were filled with dates, notes, and even a few diagrams. "My daddy started keeping this notebook right after the first time he heard about the black van. Every incident that he worked is documented here. And when he retired, he passed it on to me. But he kept on looking for that van. Kept looking right up until the day he fell over dead from a heart attack. You folks are lucky. Some folks were sitting in their car when the van hit them. A couple from Ole Miss got killed on that exact stretch of road not two years ago. We filed it as a hit and run—same as we'll do with you folks—only because 'ghost car' won't do.

Wish I could tell y'all who or what it was, but I can't. I can only tell you that this isn't the first time this has happened, and it probably won't be the last."

As Barry and Kate sat there in confused, stunned silence and listened to the trooper, Kate recalled that, before the van hit their car, the driver had thrown his head back and screamed. And the scream was like nothing she'd ever heard before.

Bogue Chitto Swamp
Pearl River County, Mississippi

Well, that's not weird," said Matt to himself as he drove past the odd-looking elderly man on the side of the road. Sure, there was nothing inherently weird about seeing someone on the side of a lonely road, but, still, something seemed off about him. He was wearing a black suit in the middle of summer, and he'd topped off this suit with a tall black hat, which he took off and waved at Matt as he drove by.

Driving past the old man, Matt glanced in his rearview mirror. The man had stopped waving his hat around and was now standing completely still and watching as Matt's car continued down the road.

"If you're wanting a ride," Matt said aloud, "it's probably best not to dress like a mortician from the 1800s." He chuckled to himself, skipped to another song on his iPhone, and continued on his way. The old man, still standing perfectly still, faded into the distance.

Matt was traveling to meet his new girlfriend's parents for the first time. He met Jennifer during their freshman year at college and had been dating her for few months. It was getting serious, he supposed; she had invited him to visit her at her parents' home during the fall break. And while Matt was looking forward to getting away from campus for a few days and enjoying some home cooking, he was somewhat nervous about meeting Jennifer's folks.

She told him that her parents lived in the country. Based on the road he was driving, which ran near the Bogue Chitto swamp in Pearl River County, Matt was pretty sure she meant in the absolute middle of countrified nowhere. The first part of his drive from school had been fine, as he cruised down the four-lane blacktop. Now, he found himself on a narrow two-lane highway that was in desperate need of maintenance. Each side of the road was surrounded by thick woods that crept up to the edge of the highway.

"Man, she wasn't lying when she said they lived in the country," Matt said, as he followed the directions on his GPS. "This is some *Hills Have Eyes* territory. Leatherface country and crap."

According to his GPS, he would be on this road for another 60 miles before the emotionless voice of his computerized navigator would tell him to turn. He shifted in his seat to get more comfortable and pressed onward.

It was several miles later that he saw the old man in the black suit again. This time he was standing closer to the road than before, with his arm extended and his thumb up. Although it was impossible, Matt was sure this was the same man he'd seen several miles back.

His tall black hat was perched on his head this time, but he was still dressed like he was in charge of a funeral in a Charles Dickens novel.

"No. Friggin'. Way . . ." Matt muttered, as he slowed his car to get a better look at the gaunt figure on the side of the road.

The man was indeed old. Very old. He was almost unnaturally thin, and his wrinkled, liver-spotted skin was stretched tight over his thin frame. His face was almost skull-like. Matt was reminded of someone suffering from a terminal disease and how they become more skeletal toward the end, just bones draped in discolored tight skin. His dark eyes were set back in their sockets and topped with long scraggly eyebrows that looked like masses of cobwebs. The same wild white hair cascaded from under his top hat and down to his shoulders. Dry, cracked lips parted into a smile that was full of long, yellow teeth with the gums receding back to the bone.

As Matt drove past, the old man leaned forward and stuck his crooked upturned thumb farther out. His grotesque smile, which Matt thought couldn't get bigger or more gross, got worse. The man was straining to smile as wide as he could, showing all of his awful teeth; his eyes were so wide with the effort that Matt could see the yellowed whites that surrounded his dark pupils and could swear they were watering. When the car was side by side with the old man, he started to shuffle to the car and reach for the passenger door.

That's when Matt floored it.

Matt saw the old man several more times. Always standing on the side of the road with his aged eyes fixed on Matt's car as it approached. Once he was standing on the side of the road and waving a stick over his head like some hellfire-spitting tent revival preacher with a Bible over his head. Another time he could swear the man was dancing or something close to it. As he drove past the old man, he was kicking up his legs and waving his arms over his head. Each time Matt saw the man on the side of the road, he went past him a little bit faster than before. He was getting scared now, and he wasn't ashamed to admit it.

The last time Matt saw the skeletal roadside figure, he cradled something bloody in his hands and held whatever it was close to his chest. This was also the moment Matt's car stopped working. His car was new—a graduation present from his folks—and had never had any trouble. But just as he passed the old man, everything on the car shut off. All the lights on the dash blinked off, his radio went dead, the AC stopped churning out cold air, and the power steering stopped working, making the steering wheel heavy and sluggish. Even his iPhone had gone dead.

As the car slowly coasted to a halt in the middle of the road, Matt turned in his seat to look behind him. The old man, still hugging something bloody close to his chest, had started hobbling toward the car. He could barely lift his feet, and each time he slid one scuffed-up black shoe forward, he kicked up a cloud of red dust.

The man's face had changed too. While still skeletal, it now looked more angular. Meaner. His wild eyes were now narrowed, beady and dark like black marbles, and they appeared to have sunken deeper into his skull, but they stayed locked on Matt. Sharp cheekbones protruded from the sides of his face, and his cheeks hugged close to the bone. His smile was still hideously large and full of long, discolored teeth. Matt watched as his mouth slowly opened and a moldy looking tongue licked his cracked, bleeding lips. The man looked more like a wolf than a man. The shuffling figure was almost to the trunk of the car now, and Matt was able to see what the old man was holding in his hands. It appeared to be the carcass of a rabbit. From the looks of the mass of blood and fur, it had died a very violent death.

Matt turned in his seat and tried the car again. He heard something touch the trunk of his car and thought he could hear the man mumbling something. Just as he was about to ditch his car and take off running on foot, the car roared to life. All the lights on the dashboard flashed on and the radio blared the song he'd just been listening to. With a loud screech, Matt peeled off and sped down the highway. He looked in his rearview mirror, expecting to see the old man still shuffling after him or throwing the dead rabbit at his car. But the highway was empty. Just a barren strip of asphalt that cut through the swamp woods like a scar.

Almost an hour later, Matt arrived at the house belonging to his girlfriend's parents. It was shortly after dark, and Matt was still shaken from his encounter but did his best to hide it. It was a lovely home, and—just like she described—it was in the middle of nowhere. Jennifer met him on the front porch.

Her parents seemed to like him and asked him all manner of questions over the course of supper. Matt did a good job of endearing himself to them and, despite what he'd been through, managed to come across as very charming. Jennifer gave him a look that let him know he was doing a good job with her parents and making quite the impression.

After supper, Matt excused himself and stepped outside. He stood quietly on the front porch and gazed at the dark woods that surrounded the house as he thought about the day's events; he'd told no one. After a few minutes, Jennifer's father came out onto the porch with two beers and gave one to Matt. They sat and made pleasant small talk. They asked about each other's families, talked sports and plans for the future. Her father offered another beer and Matt gladly accepted.

Midway through this second beer, Matt, relaxed by the alcohol, told Jennifer's father of the events that had taken place on the way there. About the old man and how he kept appearing all along the road and the sinister turn it had taken toward the end. Her father listened silently. When Matt was done with his story, the father sat there as if he was thinking of what to say in response to the outlandish report he'd just heard. Matt, despite every word of his tale being true, felt foolish.

"Matt," the father finally said. "That's what folks call an urban legend. At least that's what I think I read on the internet that it's called. I guess in this case it would be a rural legend," the father said with a chuckle. "They's always been stories about that old man haunting the roads around here for as long as I can remember."

"So you don't believe me?" asked Matt.

"Matt, nobody is going to believe you when it comes to that story. So I'd keep it to yourself." The father paused here and sat silently for a bit. After a minute or two, he spoke. "But I believe you. As sure as we're sittin' here. I saw the old man, too, one time. Back in 1965. Like to have scared me to death; I'm sure it must've done the same to you. I even saw the dead rabbit he was carrying."

Matt suddenly realized that in the excitement of telling the story, he'd omitted the detail that the old man had been holding the dead rabbit like a mother would hold a baby. The two silently stared into the darkness for a short while. And then, with a nod from Jennifer's father, they both headed inside.

Burnt Bridge Road
Hattiesburg, Mississippi

I'm pretty sure everyone has a prom night story. Prom night is one of those special nights in a person's life that mark the end of one part and the beginning of another. For many people, it's one of the last big flings with the friends they've grown up with—before life makes other plans and scatters everyone. I have a prom night story too. Mine's a bit different, I suppose, as I didn't attend my prom.

I didn't have a date for prom. So I did what most kids without dates on prom night do—I drove around and felt sorry for myself. In high school, I was a glasses-wearing nerd who was more into comic books and Dungeons and Dragons than I was football or pep rallies. I was picked on all through school and, honestly, couldn't wait to leave my hometown for the larger world. This was years before it was suddenly cool to be into geeky things. I'm still not sure how that transition happened. I blame *The Big Bang Theory*.

So, on my prom night, I was just another four-eyed, acne-covered, miserable kid driving around aimlessly, listening to even more miserable music. I think it was The Cure, but it could've been The Smiths. Yes, now that I pause to think about it, it probably was The Smiths. I was that miserable.

Initially, I drove around my hometown of Hattiesburg, but, after seeing so many of my classmates heading to the dance, I decided to get out of town and hit some of the country roads. Seeing the people I went to school with—some of whom were absolutely awful to me—all dressed up and laughing wasn't helping my mood. I just wanted to get away from everyone and drive around in the dark for a while. I tried to cheer myself up with the thought that I would be off to college in the fall and would never have to see any of these people again.

It was nearing midnight when I made it to Burnt Bridge Road. I was getting tired and figured that, after I crossed the bridge, I would find a spot to turn around and then head back to my house where I'd read comic books until I fell asleep. But as I started across the bridge, that's when I noticed something odd.

There was something on my car.

At first, I thought that it was some kind of mechanical issue. A pink-colored mist hovered over the hood. I figured I had blown some kind of gasket or a hose had come loose. As I watched, the mist got thicker and thicker. Translucent at first, the mist swirled and churned. Its color increased in brightness until I could barely see through it.

As I slowed my car and prepared for all my warning lights to pop on, something very strange happened.

The mist began to take the shape of a girl. Maybe my eyes were playing tricks on me, or something in my subconscious had taken my loneliness and channeled it into the vision in front of me, but I swear there was a girl forming on the hood of my car. The mist continued to move around, and soon I could make out more defined features. She was wearing some kind of frilly formal dress and on her wrist was something that looked like a flower. Her hair was an older-style haircut like you'd see on *Leave It to Beaver*.

I brought my car to a stop as I neared the end of the bridge, and the phantom girl slowly turned to look at me. She stared directly at me; the look on her face was one of complete sadness. She looked at me for a moment and then slowly turned her head away. When she turned, slight tendrils of pink mist followed her head, vanishing in the nighttime air.

After a moment, she glanced back over her shoulder and then slowly turned to face me. As I watched, her face began to change. Black lines began to form and spread over her. Her expression, which had been one of heartbreak and sadness, slowly contorted into an awkward grimace. For a moment I could swear she was silently trying to scream as she continued to turn completely black. She gritted her teeth together, her eyes wide and crazy with some kind of phantom pain. Making eye contact with me one last time—her face as black as tar—it was then that I made a ghastly realization.

She's burning, I thought.

And then she was gone.

I sat there for a few moments, shaken and wondering about what I'd seen. Or thought I'd seen. I also wondered if I was having a stroke or hallucinating. Once I managed to calm myself down and was sure I wasn't suffering from some kind of brain issue, I turned my car around and drove home in silence. My hands gripped the steering wheel so tightly that they ached the next day.

I never told anyone what happened that night. Not my parents. And not the few friends I did have. They wouldn't believe me, of that I was sure. They would chalk it up to a cry for attention or just my overactive imagination running wild. In time, I started to doubt my own memories of the night.

The school year ended; the following fall, I was off to college. I really came into my own there. I found a group of friends who were into the same things I was. I eventually managed to get myself a serious girlfriend. We're still together as of this writing and planning to get married soon. I majored in creative writing and, as an elective, took an anthropology course on folklore. I figured I would get some ideas for my stories from that class. One of our assignments was to write about local folklore in our hometown. And that's where I learned about the ghost of Burnt Bridge Road.

There are several variations on the origin of the ghost that supposedly haunts Burnt Bridge Road. Some say she's the ghost of a girl who was murdered on the night of the prom. Others say that she and her boyfriend were killed on the night of their prom when the car they were in careened off the bridge and burst into flames. That's the one I tend to believe. After all, I saw her burn.

I've driven that road several times since then, and I haven't seen anything out of the ordinary again. But I know that, on that night several years ago, the night I didn't go to my own prom, I saw something out there on that lonely strip of road. And I'm sure it was the ghost of a girl who never got to tell her own prom night story.

The Eola Hotel
Natchez, Mississippi

Blake Harrison had just started as the new bartender at the elegant Eola Hotel in Natchez, and it was a slow night. The bar had a few of what Blake assumed were regulars sitting around nursing their drinks, but, overall, business was dead. That was OK with Blake, as he needed time to familiarize himself with the bar, even though he'd miss the tip money that he relied on.

Blake had noticed that Tuesday nights were usually like this in the bartending world. On Monday nights, people wanted to drink simply because it was Monday night and the start of a new workweek. People drank on Wednesday nights to celebrate the ending of the middle of the week, on Thursdays because it was the eve of the weekend, and then people drank on the weekend to celebrate the end of another workweek. But drinking on Tuesday nights? That generic, bland evening served no purpose at all, so it was always dead.

After putting some glasses away and familiarizing himself with the locations of various spirits, Blake turned to see a middle-aged gentleman standing at the bar. His hands were resting on the counter, and he was staring straight ahead at the wall of bottles in front of him. He was dressed in a three-button tweed suit with a matching vest and a high, stiff collar.

Truthfully, Blake didn't think too much of the man's odd attire. He chalked it up to what he called the *Downton Abbey* effect. Since that show had aired on PBS, more and more people had started wearing clothes based on fashion from the 1920s and 30s. A bunch of Blake's hipster friends were doing it nowadays as well.

Personally, he liked the new trend. He would rather have a bar full of people dressed like this than wearing some goofy graphic T-shirt, shorts, and flip-flops. Or, Blake figured, the man could've been a part of some historical tour where the guides dressed like people from the past. That happened a lot in the historic district. Whatever it was, Blake was happy for the company and the potential tip.

"Give me a scotch and soda, son," the man said.

"Sure thing," Blake said, with a well-practiced smile. "One scotch and soda coming right up."

The man didn't reply. He only continued to stare straight ahead. Blake turned and grabbed a bottle of Johnny Walker and proceeded to mix the man's drink. Although some of the tables had customers sitting at them, no one was sitting at the bar.

"I gotta say, I'm glad you stopped by," Blake said over his shoulder to the man. "I was starting to get lonesome up here. Tuesday nights are always dead."

"...always dead...," said the man in a flat, hollow voice. His voice sounded distracted, distant.

"Yeah, that's what I said," Blake replied, as he turned around. "Here ya go. One scotch and soda. You wanna start a tab?"

The man was gone. The only people in the bar were Blake and the bleary-eyed regulars. Puzzled, Blake walked out from around the bar and looked for the strange man who had ordered a drink and then, as weird as it seemed, simply vanished. There was no sign of him. Blake left the drink on the bar in case the man returned, and then he went back to work.

"So, how was your first night?" Blake's manager asked, as they made their way out of the hotel.

"Not too bad. I think I'm going to like working here. It was pretty quiet tonight. But ya know, it's a Tuesday. It happens."

"Oh, it will pick up, I assure you. We are one of the best places for a drink in Natchez. I think you'll enjoy it here," his manager said with a smile.

Before he could reply, a portrait on the wall in the hallway caught Blake's eye. He stopped to get a better look at it.

"Um, who is this?" Blake asked, as he looked at the picture in front of him.

"That," said the manager, "is Mr. Isidore Levy. He was one of the original developers and financiers of the Eola hotel. It's actually named after his daughter. He opened this place in 1927. His daughter passed away right before the grand opening. A sad affair, I'm sure. Unfortunately, he was hit hard by the stock market crash of 1929 and the hotel was sold. I want to say he passed away in the 1950s. Why do you ask?"

"Because I'm pretty sure he ordered a drink from me tonight," said Blake, as he continued to stare at the portrait on the wall.

Rowland
Medical Library
Jackson, Mississippi

I left the Rowland Medical Library a little after midnight, knowing that there was no way I was going to pass my exam the following day. No matter how much I crammed, prayed, or came up with little ways to remember various medical facts, I was doomed. I also wondered if I would even be a part of the 1995 graduating class because a lot was hanging on this particular test.

I pulled my coat tight, hoisted my backpack up on my shoulder, and began the walk to my car. I figured at this point, a good night's sleep would probably be more effective than any more caffeine-fueled study binges. Sometimes you just have to give in and let the chips fall where they may.

The campus of the University of Mississippi Medical Center in Jackson was pretty dead, with most students sequestered away behind piles of books and notes. The students who were out on this fall night silently shuffled across campus, rarely acknowledging each other's presence as they passed. They looked more like shell-shocked soldiers returning from some muddy, bloody battlefield than medical students.

Overhead, the moon occasionally peeked out from the dark, bloated clouds above and bathed the campus in its pale light. All in all, it was a perfect fall night, one that reminded me of high school football games, bonfires, and trick-or-treating. It definitely wasn't a night for studying.

I crossed a side street and made my way to the parking lot where my beat-up car was located. The lot was completely empty except for my little silver Nissan, which waited for me under one of the lights. I've always found it eerie when my car is the only one in a parking lot. Maybe I've watched too many episodes of *Unsolved Mysteries*. Seems like a lot of people have vanished from empty parking lots that, in reality, weren't always quite so empty.

As I dug in my pocket for my keys, I glanced over at a small stand of pine trees and did a double take at what I saw. At the edge of the trees was a figure pacing back and forth. It took exactly 10 steps forward, turned, and then took 10 steps back. The figure's head was bowed, and it wore some kind of loose-fitting gown that fluttered in the breeze. I kept staring at the strange figure as it followed the same walking pattern over and over. Long, stringy hair cascaded over its face like some kind of greasy veil, and I couldn't tell if it was male or female. Either way, it was extremely thin. Sickly. And it never broke from its 10-step routine. Over and over, it took 10 steps forward and back, arms slack, head bobbing with each repeated step.

At first, I thought it might be someone who was part of a live-action role-playing organization on campus. Every now and then, while walking across campus at night, you'd see some student chasing another with a cardboard stake or whacking some other student with a large foam sword. Those guys always cracked me up, but, hey, do what you want to do, right? Still, this figure never acknowledged my presence and kept up the same routine for several minutes. Hell, maybe it was some medical student who had snapped under the pressure and was now wandering around campus in a catatonic state. Believe it or not, stuff like that happens in med school.

Finally, my curiosity got the better of me, and I called out to the figure, just to see if I would get any kind of reaction.

"Ya know, you keep that up and you're gonna wear a rut in the grass," I said. Nothing. Just 10 steps forward, turn, 10 steps back. I stepped a bit closer and tried to get a better look at the mysterious figure. It was wearing some kind of shabby, tattered gown. Thin, emaciated legs protruded from the bottom and there were no shoes of any sort. Man, those feet had to be cold. "Or...you know....just keep doing...whatever it is you're... doing."

I pulled out a small pen light that I carried at night for when I needed help finding the lock on my apartment door. Being somewhat of a slacker, I'd never replaced the porch bulb once it burned out. As the pen light cut through the dark, the figure stopped in its tracks. It stood perfectly still, head bowed and face hidden by a mass of greasy, straight hair. Slowly, it turned to face me and began to shuffle toward me, its bare feet dragging through the wet grass. One shoulder was hunched down, and the figure never looked up as it approached. It just kept ambling its way toward me without a word. As it came closer, the only sound it made was a raspy breathing, as if its lungs were full of something.

I instinctively backed up to my car, holding the tiny pen light in my hand. The figure shuffled onto the parking lot, its bare feet making a slapping sound on the pavement as it came closer, never looking up. This definitely wasn't some weirdo kid doing live-action anything, and it most definitely wasn't some overstressed student. As it came closer, the moon slid behind the clouds, and I swear the temperature dropped. It dropped so much that, suddenly, I could see my own breath. However, as the approaching figure plodded toward me, I noticed there was no vapor accompanying that awful rasping breath. None at all.

I froze as I leaned against my car. One hand was digging for my keys and the other was holding my pen light out like some goofy character from an old vampire movie holding up a cross. The chilled air was suddenly filled with a musky, moldy odor of wet rotted things as the figure hobbled close to me. The arms, which up until this point had been slack by its side, slowly began to rise toward me, and I noticed that its fingernails were either missing or barely hanging on by bits of bloody skin.

"HEY, NOW!" I yelled. "BACK UP!"

The figure's head raised, as its hair parted like a dirty curtain. Black, cracked lips opened to reveal jagged teeth; its skin was gray and covered in oozing scabs and sores. As its tongue writhed in its mouth, the figure began coughing up dirt, which cascaded down the front of its dingy gown. Its eyes, which were nothing more than pale-white runny orbs, fixed on me.

"GET BACK!" I screamed, as I instinctively punched forward, with my eyes shut in terror. My punch only connected with air, and, when I opened my eyes, I was alone in the parking lot. That moldy smell lingered in the air as the only reminder of what had been there. I stood there for a moment before hopping into my car and racing home.

It's been 20 years since then, and the events of that night are replaying in my head as I sit here at my desk and stare silently at the headline before me. Up to 7,000 bodies of former patients of the Mississippi State Lunatic Asylum—which closed in 1935—have recently been unearthed on the campus of the University of Mississippi Medical Center. The grounds of the medical school were originally the burial grounds for the asylum. (This is something they failed to mention in orientation.) I stare at the screen and look at the accompanying picture of rotten wooden coffins emerging from the mud and swear that a horrid moldy odor has filled the room.

The Witch of Yazoo
Yazoo City, Mississippi

Something had to be done about the old woman who lived alone on the banks of the Yazoo River. Of this, the town was certain. And in the summer of 1884, when a badly wounded fisherman staggered into town, the people decided that the time to deal with her had come.

His clothes were bloody and his body was covered in strange symbols that were gouged into his flesh. The fisherman told the townspeople gathered around that he and his companion had been fishing on the river when they were drawn to a lonely shack by cries for help. He remembered approaching the cabin with his friend, but he recalled nothing more until he awoke on the floor of the shack.

"I swear, we was just heading up to that shack and that's all I remember. I remember Bill sayin' it sounds like someone is dyin' up there and we best go help out.

We got to the door and next thing I know, I'm on the floor of the shack and in awful pain. I had all these marks on me, and Bill was hung up in a corner, dead. He'd been gutted. Like you'd do with a damn deer. Weren't nobody in the cabin. Just me and poor ol' Bill. There was a meal of some sort cookin' over the fire, so somebody had been there. I managed to get up off the floor and stagger off into the woods. Walked for a long time, and now here I am in the sorry state you see me."

The townsfolk looked at each other and cursed under their breath. A woman said a quick prayer. Another almost fainted. The people of Yazoo City had always heard stories of strange goings-on at the lone cabin on the river. Children would sometimes sneak out there at night and return to town with tales of wild screaming and singing coming from inside the shack. But this—this bloodied man with his tale of a gruesome murder—was something else.

"Somebody best get the sheriff," said Emmet Lott, who ran one of the town stores. "He'll be wantin' to know 'bout this."

Everyone nodded in agreement, and a young boy ran off to fetch the sheriff.

"You ever seen such a wicked mess, boss?" the deputy asked, as he and the sheriff walked around the shack by the river. He covered his mouth with a handkerchief as he took in the scene around him.

"I surely have not," the sheriff replied. "Not in all my days."

The interior of the shack was dark, lit only by a fire in the fireplace and a single oil lamp, and it smelled of blood and rot. Just as the fisherman had told them, the body of his friend was there in the corner, hanging from his neck by a rope. The rough rope had dug deep into his throat and was tossed over a rafter and tied off on one of the support beams for the cabin. One of his eyes was missing, and his tongue had almost been pulled completely out of his mouth. In the darkness of the cabin, the two men could hear flies buzzing.

On the wooden floor of the cabin was a large, strange symbol that neither the sheriff nor his deputy had seen before. It had been carved directly into the wood, and smaller strange symbols surrounded it. Piles of various objects were also placed neatly near the symbols. The sheriff kicked over one of the piles with the toe of his boot. The pile was made up of bird feathers, small bones, and some gray roots.

"My granddaddy had to pay a call to a hoodoo woman when I was a child. Took me with him. All this stuff on the floor reminds me of her place," said the sheriff. He spit a stream of tobacco juice into the middle of the circle on the floor and proceeded to rub it into the wood with his boot. "I still have dreams sometimes of going up in her house. Couldn't have been more'n nine. Wouldn't let go of my granddaddy's hand until he made me do so."

"I'll surely be having nightmares about this place," the deputy whispered. "You think we should go ahead and cut this poor soul down?"

"Not till we find the woman what done this," the sheriff answered.

One of the citizens who'd been deputized on the spot called out from the front porch. The old woman had walked out of the woods, seen the crowd at her cabin, and fled back into the forest. The sheriff and his deputy exchanged a quick glance and unholstered their guns. Their heavy boots shook the entire cabin as they ran out.

Lord, she is fast. Ain't natural, thought the sheriff as he pursued the old woman. She raced ahead of them at a speed that would rival any swamp rabbit. Darting under tree limbs and leaping over moss-covered logs, she ran ahead of them with her dirty clothes and stringy, filthy hair flailing behind her. The sheriff and his men did their best to try and keep up, and the old woman cackled at their efforts.

Soon, losing sight of the evil old woman, the men slowed their pursuit and continued in the direction she was last seen. All the men were gasping for air. A few crouched down, waved their hands, and said they could not go another step farther. All were soaked with sweat from running in the heat of the summer day.

One by one, all the men in the posse eventually stopped to rest. Soon, only the sheriff and his deputy were left. "You got it in you to keep goin'?" asked the sheriff of his deputy.

"I do," he replied. "I'll go as long as I can."

"S'all I can ask. Let's get at it."

The two continued for several more minutes through the thick swampy wood. Finally, with no sign of the crone or her trail, the two were on the verge of giving up. Just as they looked at each other to see who would bring up the idea of giving up the chase first, a harsh voice spoke out from the woods in front of them.

"You men best help me. You best, that's for sure, or I'll visit damnation and ruin upon you."

The two edged forward with guns drawn, walking with a cautious, deliberate pace. The ground beneath their boots got softer and softer as they approached the voice that once again demanded help. Both readied their guns. The barrel of the deputy's shotgun shook as he held it out in front of him.

The old woman was before them, slowly sinking in quicksand. Already, she was up to her neck in the thick muck. She pivoted her head and fixed her eyes on the two of them. One of her eyes was black, and the other one was the color of spoiled milk. Her matted, greasy hair fanned out around her head, and her mouth was filled with teeth that had been filed to rough points.

"Best help me," she said, in a voice that reminded them of rusty screen door hinges. "I'll damn the lot of ya, if you don't." She looked at them expectantly. The sheriff thought she looked at them hungrily too.

"Let the mud take her," was all the sheriff said.

The hag glared at the sheriff with wild eyes. She seemed lost in thought for a moment, as she slowly sank deeper. Then she spoke.

"In 20 years, I will bring destruction down upon your town and your people. I'll burn your homes and your children. My flames will eat the town up and leave blackened homes and black bones."

The sheriff spit a wad of tobacco into the quicksand as the mud finally took her.

Days later, a mule and a chain were brought out, and the townsfolk pulled the woman's body from the quicksand. They buried her in Glenwood Cemetery, where they could keep an eye on her, rather than leaving her body in the swamp. A tombstone was erected with a simple inscription of TW: The Witch. A chain was placed around the grave, as some members of the town believed this would shackle the old woman to her gravesite. And then the old woman and the story of her bloody deeds drifted into local legend and campfire stories.

In 1904, a fire broke out at the home of one Miss Wise, who was preparing for her wedding. When she recounted the fire, she claimed it seemed alive and was impervious to water and any attempts to put it out. In minutes, it engulfed her house. As townsfolk raced to try to put out the fire, a violent wind came up, unheard-of weather in May. The wind howled, pushing the flames to other structures. As the residents told it later, the flames seemed determined to burn the whole town down, and they almost succeeded at their task.

Before the fire was contained, 200 homes and businesses were reduced to ash and smoldering embers. The residents of Yazoo City stumbled around among the ruins and tried to recover as best as they could.

More than one grimy, soot-covered face glanced in the direction of Glenwood Cemetery.

The sheriff, slower than he had been 20 years before, due to the passage of time and a bootlegger's bullet that was lodged in his leg, was the first to make the trek up to the cemetery and the witch's grave. He remembered her vow that she'd made some 20 years ago, to have her revenge on the town. Was it to the day? He couldn't remember for sure.

When he arrived at the grave, he was startled to discover that the headstone was cracked down the middle and the thick rusty chain surrounding her grave was broken. The giant links seemed to have been pulled apart.

The sheriff stared at the grave for a few silent moments and was soon joined by some of the more curious residents of Yazoo City, who crept up cautiously and looked at the grave with wild eyes.

"It's a hell of a thing," he finally said.

Vicksburg
National Battlefield
Vicksburg, Mississippi

Jim Webber awoke shortly before dawn in the Confederate encampment in Vicksburg and emerged from his tent into the muggy Mississippi morning. The rest of the camp was dark, with only a few fellow soldiers up at this hour. Taking his musket from where it was stacked with several others, he made his way to a nearby campfire, lured by the smell of freshly brewed coffee. Winding through the tents, he could hear other soldiers snoring away.

There was one soldier sitting near the fire, looking down and slowly nursing a tin cup filled with steaming hot coffee. Jim, still yawning and trying to wake up, approached the campfire and sat down on a small stool. The figure sitting beside the fire didn't look up or acknowledge his arrival in any way.

"Morning, soldier," said Jim, mid-yawn. "Any more coffee left?"

The huddled figure, who was wearing the same gray uniform as Jim, didn't respond. The man kept his hands clasped around his mess kit cup and stared into the embers of the fire in front of him. Jim leaned forward on his stool and waved one of his hands in an attempt to get his fellow soldier's attention.

"Oh, sorry," the man said loudly when he noticed he had company. He set his cup down and pulled a pair of earbuds out of his ears. "Didn't see you come up." He pulled a cell phone from his jacket and tapped the screen. "Was just listening to the new Dylan album," he said with a laugh.

"I'm pretty sure they didn't have smartphones and earbuds in 1863."

"Show hasn't started yet," the man replied sheepishly, referring to the reenactment that they, along with several hundred other Civil War history enthusiasts, would be putting on later today. "Once the day's festivities commence, I promise I'll be 100% historically accurate."

"No worries," Jim said with a laugh. "I had my Kindle out in my tent last night. Just can't let go of some of our modern conveniences."

"Ain't that the truth? You want some coffee?"

"Want *and* need. I didn't sleep for squat last night. Too dang hot. I must've tossed and turned all night." Jim pulled out his knapsack and began rummaging around for the tin coffee cup he'd picked up off eBay a while back. "Now, where did I put that thing?" he muttered to himself.

His fellow reenactor watched silently as Jim moved the contents of his knapsack around in search of his cup. After he had done everything but upend his knapsack, Jim came to the realization that he must have left his cup back at his tent.

"Well, shoot," he said. "I gotta run back to my tent. Left my cup there. I'll be right back. Save some coffee for me."

"Will do," the other man said, as Jim got up and began trudging back the way he'd come.

Had the sun not been starting to creep over the horizon, Jim would've taken his own phone out and used the flashlight app to help navigate. The last thing he wanted to do was trip over some soldier's bundle, and he would never hear the end of it if he plowed into one of the musket stacks that the reenactors kept outside their tents. The tripod stacks gave everything more of an air of authenticity, even if it wasn't the safest thing when it came to walking around at night.

As he walked back to his tent, Jim managed to almost run into another soldier. The man seemed to come out of nowhere. He was dressed in a similar gray Confederate uniform, only his heavy woolen jacket was unbuttoned and slightly open down the front. A musket was slung over one shoulder, his bayonet fixed to the barrel. It pointed in the air like a spire and was a clear violation of camp rules.

"Oh, sorry," Jim apologized. "Didn't see you there. Still waking up. I'm worthless without my morning coffee. Say, you might want to unfix that bayonet. Don't want to stick somebody with that thing."

The soldier, who had walked past Jim, stopped and slowly turned. His uniform was beat all to hell and was covered in patches and other homemade repairs. A heavy bedroll was draped over his other shoulder and tied off at the ends, and his mess kit quietly rattled as he turned around. The dingy cap on his head was pulled low and, beneath it, a scraggly beard cascaded down. His skin was blackened and dirty. This guy was clearly going for realism in his outfit.

"Whoa," said Jim. "That is some outfit. Well done." He paused. Was that gunpowder he was smelling mingled in with the strong smell of body odor? "I mean that is really well put together."

As Jim spoke, the soldier slowly opened the front of his wool jacket to reveal his chest, which was covered in blood. The man was silent as he did this but appeared to be trying to speak. He opened and closed his mouth like a fish tossed onto a riverbank. Most of his teeth were missing, and the few that remained were rotten and discolored. His eyes were bloodshot, and trails of moisture cut through the grime on his face. As he staggered forward, Jim could see a gaping wound in his stomach. The blood had coagulated on his shirt, and the wound was framed in an awful ring of dried blood.

Jim tried to speak, but the words stuck in his throat as the bloody soldier shambled toward him.

Gut shot. That man's been gut shot.

"Hold on, buddy." Jim finally managed to stutter. "You need some help. There's a guy in one of the artillery units who is a doctor." Jim glanced over his shoulder toward the main camp where the doctor would be. He tried to mentally gauge how quickly he could make it over there and back with the doctor in tow. "Let me help you down and uh . . . I'll go get some help."

When Jim turned back around, he was alone. The bloody soldier was gone. He didn't know how long he stood there, shocked at what he'd just seen. When he came back to his senses, the camp was starting to wake up and the smell of coffee and cooking fatback wafted lightly through the air. Underneath the enticing aroma of breakfast, Jim could smell the faint hint of gunpowder. It lingered in the air for a few brief moments and then dissipated in the early morning summer breeze.

Longwood House
Natchez, Mississippi

The boy had fresh pralines, and that was good. He was also on his second house of the tour in a day filled with house tours in Natchez, and that was bad. His dad loved old houses. The older, the better. He would walk around these homes in a semi-daze as he marveled at the quality of the woodwork. Homes built before the Civil War were his dad's favorites.

The boy, on the other hand, didn't think too much of old houses. Old houses were just that—houses that were old. Sure, some of the high ceilings and creaky staircases were cool and reminded him of Harry Potter, but soon his interest faded, and the boy would be left to his own devices as his dad wandered around and studied the structures in great detail.

To make matters worse, this particular house wasn't even finished. On the outside, it looked like a Southern palace made of porches, high windows, and an actual dome on top. The boy had to admit that was pretty neat.

He imagined a wizard living up there, casting spells by starlight. But once they were inside, the boy learned that the house wasn't even done. Only the basement was compete. The rest looked more like the backside of a movie set rather than an actual home.

The tour guide explained, " . . . and when the war broke out, the workers stopped whatever they were doing and fled north to prepare for the oncoming conflict. Legend has it, their tools remained for years in the exact spots where they dropped them. Due to the war, the house was never finished and eventually fell into ruin."

Everyone craned their necks as the tour guide carried on: "During the war, the family lived in the basement, as it was the only completed level of the home. Dr. Haller Nutt died before the war's end in 1864. The official cause of death was pneumonia, but most people say he died of a broken heart over the state of his finances and, most importantly, his unfinished home. His wife, Julia, continued to live here in the basement at Longwood until her own death in 1897."

The boy sighed loud enough to get shushed by his father and to be on the receiving end of more than a few dirty looks from the other people on the tour. All these names and dates were boring. Old houses were boring. Adults were boring. Everything about this trip was boring, and this was no way to spend a Saturday afternoon. At least outside he could be on his own and go exploring. The boy left the main group in the dining room as the tour guide was explaining the manually operated fan that hung above the table.

He started heading for the front door when he first saw the woman. She appeared out of the corner of his eye and moved silently across the opening to the adjacent room, pausing as the boy turned to look at her. The woman was dressed in a faded yellow hoop skirt adorned with an even more faded floral pattern. Her skin was a milky white, her hair pulled back in a tight bun. She silently moved about the room and did not acknowledge the boy's presence. She occasionally paused to look at some of the various wall hangings.

After a moment or two, the woman made eye contact with the boy. She was very pretty, the boy thought, but there was an air of sadness about her. Her face was stoic, but, still, there was something about her eyes. She gazed up at the unfinished levels above her as if she were able to see through the many floors and all the way up into the top dome. She stared for a bit, looked back at the boy, and seemed to sigh. With that, she disappeared into an adjacent room. She moved silently and, as the boy would later recall, seemed to actually glide.

Leaving the cavernous house, the boy stepped out into the bright sunshine to explore the grounds. The humid air was thick with the smells of summer. While not nearly as crowded outside, several people milled about the gardens.

In the garden, the boy noticed yet another figure who seemed out of place. A man was pacing back and forth with his hands clasped behind his back and his head lowered in deep thought. He, like the woman the boy had seen earlier, was dressed in what appeared to be Civil War–era clothing and looked as though he'd just stepped off the set of *Gone with the Wind*. His mother loved that movie and would occasionally talk the boy into watching it with her.

That's it, the boy thought. These are actors. They must be doing some kind of reenactment thing here at the house today.

He watched the man pace back and forth a little longer. A chattering young couple walked right past the man without noticing him. They didn't stop to speak with him or ask him who he was dressed up as. In fact, it was almost like they didn't see him at all. Several other tourists passed the man as well. The boy figured that these people and their costumes had to be a pretty normal occurrence here at Longwood because no one seemed to think they were out of place. Tired of watching the man, the boy took off to explore the rest of the grounds.

Later, the boy found his father speaking to the woman who was acting as the tour guide. The boy hoped he could drag his dad away so they could be on the road soon, as he didn't want to miss his Saturday night TV shows. If the boy didn't drop hints to his father that it was time to go, they would be here past nightfall.

"Well, there he is," his father said as he turned to look at his son. "Where ya been?"

"Oh, just exploring," the boy replied. "I hung around inside and then needed some fresh air. I saw the actors you guys have here. What are they gonna do today?"

The woman made a face as if something was out of place, that something was odd. "Honey," the woman said. "There's no actors here today. I'm the only one on duty."

"But I saw them. There was a woman in the house and some guy walking around in the garden. They looked like they were dressed up to play a part."

"Son," the boy's father chimed in. "What are you talking about?"

"I think I know," said the tour guide. "Those weren't actors, sweetie. I've seen them too. It's rare to see them, but people sometimes do. It's very rare to see them both in the same day. First time I think that's happened."

"I'm sorry," the father interjected. "But what exactly are you talking about?"

The boy was silent as the tour guide crouched down until she was at eye level with him. She gently reached out and placed both hands on his shoulders.

"What you saw weren't actors or tour guides dressed up in period costumes. Now, we do have those, but only during pilgrimage time. What you saw were Mr. and Mrs. Nutt. Or at least the part of them that stays at the house. You see, the original owners of the house, they're still. . . " She paused, ". . . here."

"Even though they both died, they never really left this house. Their heartbreak at never having finished their dream home was so intense and terrible that it sort of bound them to the house forever. Doctors can tell you the medical term for what they died of, but everyone that knew them said it was a broken heart over this house never being finished and having to live in the basement. At one point, the house was even referred to as Nutt's Folly. Usually people just report a feeling of being watched. Sometimes people say they smell Mrs. Nutt's perfume. People have reported seeing them. But never both on one day. That's a new one. You are one special little boy."

The father stifled a chuckle. "OK, kiddo, we need to get on the road. Your mom will kill us if I bring you home late." He didn't have time for ghosts or hauntings. He was only interested in things he could physically touch—the banister of a staircase, the molding of a door frame, and things of that nature. The unseen world that lurked beyond our normal one was of no interest to him. But it was to the boy. That night, as they drove home in darkness, the boy reclined on the backseat of his father's car. Ernest Tubb played on the radio, while the boy thought of the grand unfinished house and the heartbroken husband and wife who were still there after all these years. Anchored to the house by their despair and, like the house itself, stuck in time. Soon the boy drifted off to sleep. When they got home, his father gently carried him inside and tucked him into bed.

Nash Road (Three-Legged Lady Road)
Columbus, Mississippi

"Go ahead. Turn the lights off."

Jay sat in his parked car and nervously gripped the steering wheel a little tighter. His eyes strained when he peered into the darkness. The girl in the passenger seat looked at him expectantly, daring him to turn off the car's lights, to see if the legend of Three-Legged Lady Road was true or not. Now that he was out here on this lonesome road, surrounded by scraggly trees and darkness you can only find in the backcountry, Jay wasn't sure if he wanted to find out.

How did I get myself into this? Jay thought to himself.

It started simply enough, at a bar called The Landing in Columbus. Over beers and shots, the topic of Three-Legged Lady Road and the ghost that supposedly haunted it had come up. No one could agree on the origins. Like most local legends, the details were varied and changed over time.

"Well," one of Jay's friends had said. "Technically, it's called Nash Road, but the locals all call it Three-Legged Lady Road on account of the ghost that haunts it."

"Three-Legged Lady Road? Ghost? What are you guys even talking about?" said Chelsea, rolling her eyes.

Some said the ghost was the mother of a young girl who was murdered and subsequently dismembered on the road. When the mother went to look for her daughter, all she could find was a severed leg. The mother was said to haunt the road while carrying the bloody, tattered leg in an eternal quest to find her daughter—or what was left of her.

Others attributed the ghost to the story of a farmer's wife who discovered her husband was having an affair. In a fury, she hacked him to pieces with an ax as he slept. Driven mad by her rage, she sewed his severed leg to her own hip so they would always be together. Jay and his friends agreed this one was a little far-fetched. Still, they all believed *something* was out there on that lonely strip of road. Well, everyone except Jay's new girlfriend, Chelsea.

"You have got to be kidding me," she'd said while Jay and his friends discussed the local legend. "You people actually believe this stuff?"

Of course they believed it. Jay and his friends had heard about the ghost of Three-Legged Lady Road all their lives. From stories told around campfires and Halloween parties to tales whispered between friends about trips out to the road, the ghost was a part of their lives and had been for as long as Jay could remember. Even his folks talked about it. Chelsea, who had moved to the area to attend Mississippi State, was a bit more jaded when it came to stories of ghost mothers and severed legs.

"Well, Chelsea," said another of Jay's friends. "If you don't believe it, why don't you and Jay go out there tonight?"

Jay nearly choked on his beer, while Chelsea laughed and said that was an awesome idea.

"Oh, come on, Jay," Chelsea pined. "Kill the lights. That's supposed to bring her out, isn't it? I wonder if she'll be all bloody and gross? Honk the horn, kill the lights. Let's give the ghost . . . a leg up." She laughed.

"Not funny," Jay replied nervously. To tell the truth, Jay was a little more than nervous. He didn't think it would be this bad. Sure, he thought he would be a little skittish, but he was genuinely afraid. Thinking he saw something move beyond the glow of his headlights, Jay squinted into the darkness. Gazing into the shadowed woods, he suddenly realized he really didn't want to turn the headlights off.

Chelsea turned in the passenger seat to face him and began playing with his hair. "Oh, come on," she teased. "There's nothing out there. Maybe an owl and a possum or two. But no ghost lady with a severed leg or a sewn-on leg, for that matter. Just kill the lights. Only for a second. For . . . me."

Jay glanced at Chelsea. She had inched closer to him and was leaning in slowly.

"You really must want to see this ghost," Jay stammered as he leaned toward her.

"Oh, I'm not interested in any ghosts, boyo." She whispered as she drew him near. As their lips met, Jay flipped the headlights off. She sighed as she moved into his kiss.

A loud knock on the roof of the car startled them both. It was a sharp sound. Deliberate. Chelsea jumped with a confused look on her face as she glanced at the roof of the car. The knock didn't sound like anything had fallen on the car. Outside the car, shrouded in darkness, they could hear something slowly crunching through the leaves.

"What the hell was that?" Chelsea asked. "Are your idiot friends out there? If they are…"

"I swear, I have no idea what that was," Jay replied. "The guys all went back to the dorm."

Another loud knock reverberated through the car. This one louder and more forceful. It was followed by another. And another. Each knock was harder than the last, until the car was shaking. Jay flipped on the headlights and watched in horror as a shadowy figure disappeared into the surrounding woods. Although he couldn't make out much, he could see that the figure was hunched over as if it was carrying something.

"OK, we're out of here," he said, as he cranked the car and stomped on the gas pedal.

Chelsea gazed out the passenger window into the darkness as the car began to move.

"There's somebody out there!" She screamed and recoiled from the window. Later she would describe the stooped, swaying figure to Jay's friends and how, even though she couldn't see its face, she knew it was looking straight at her.

Jay's car kicked up gravel as it tore down Three-Legged Lady Road and Chelsea let out a yelp as something rammed into the side of the car. Jay pulled the steering wheel hard to the right to keep his car on the road. The tires slid on the loose rock as he fought to keep the car from running into the ditch that ran alongside them.

"What the hell was that?!" he yelled. The car jolted to the left again as an unseen force attempted to push it off the road.

"There's nothing out there!" Chelsea cried as the car jolted to the left again with a hollow thud.

Get to the end of the road. That's how it works, isn't it? That's what they always said in the stories. Get to the end of the road and she can't get you, Jay thought as he fought with the steering wheel.

Over and over, something slammed into the passenger side of the car with a loud booming thud, causing the vehicle to shake. As Chelsea let out another scream, Jay's only thought was that something out there in the darkness was trying to kill them.

Jay's car raced down the narrow, winding road, roaring past the woods, which were just a dark, black blur. Chelsea slid over to Jay's side of the car and placed her hands on the passenger door to brace herself, as the car shook and skidded each time the unseen violent force slammed into it. She let out a final scream as Jay rounded the last turn before exiting Three-Legged Lady Road. The car was rocked one last time by whatever was out there. The final hit was so hard, Jay could've sworn the car went up on two wheels. They fishtailed onto the main road that led into town and disappeared into the night.

When they arrived at Chelsea's dorm, she leapt out of the car, still shaken over what had happened. Jay opened his door and called out for her to wait. She stopped her mad dash to the dorm and turned around. But when she saw the massive number of dents on her side of the car, she spun back around and sprinted to the dorm without saying a word.

The Merrehope House
Meridian, Mississippi

It was near closing time when Frank Merit burst into the office of H&H Contractors. The look on his face told his boss, Sam, that he wouldn't be getting off at the usual closing time. Instead of heading home to supper, Sam would more than likely be dealing with whatever was bothering Frank. Another late day at the office.

"I ain't going back to that house," Frank said firmly.

"What house? The Merrehope house? That's where you're working, right?" Sam asked as he pushed a pile of invoices aside.

"Was working," Frank replied, correcting him. "Was working. Like I said, I ain't going back."

"What the hell happened?" asked Sam. It wasn't like Frank to walk off a job like this.

"You ain't gonna believe me."

"Humor me," Sam said.

Frank paced the office for a bit. Then he sat down. After a few more awkward moments, he told his story. The Merrehope home was one of the finest in Meridian, Mississippi. The 26-room mansion was constructed in 1858. It miraculously survived the Civil War and was spared Sherman's torch. A historical museum filled with antiques, it drew visitors from all over the world and looked just as stately as ever. However, the mansion tended to show its age at times; when that happened, contractors like Frank were called in.

Frank loved working on these old houses. Modern houses felt cheap, like products off an assembly line— no more unique than a Toyota. There was no trace of the builder in the woodwork. No personal touch and no personality. These old houses were works of art. In Frank's mind, modern houses were nothing more than generic, disposable structures.

Earlier that day, the lady on duty at the house had let Frank in and explained that she had to step out to go pick her child up from school, so Frank would be on his own. She took him on a brief tour of the areas of the house that needed some work, explained there were snacks and drinks in the fridge, and then left. Frank lugged his tools in and decided to start working on some molding that had become loose.

Frank had been working for about an hour when, strangely enough, he heard what sounded like footsteps upstairs. These old houses creaked a lot. They creaked even more when someone was walking on the floor above. Frank paused his work and listened. The footsteps, if indeed they were footsteps, were very faint. But that's what it sounded like, like someone pacing around in one of the upstairs rooms. The rhythmic creaking of the aged floorboards was quiet. But it was there.

Stopping his work completely, Frank took some time to search upstairs. The caretaker had told him they were the only ones in the house and he had no cause to doubt her. But still, he'd heard what he heard. After a cursory check of the upstairs, including the closets and even under a bed or two, Frank chalked it up to his imagination. Old houses made noises. They creaked and groaned regularly, just like old bones.

Heading back to the stairs, Frank paused again and listened. There was something else. He could hear what he would describe as—for lack of a better word— mumbling. It was definitely the sound of someone talking in a faint deep voice, but he couldn't make out a word. It reminded him of what folks in the radio business call "bleed over"—where one frequency bleeds over to another one. Just this strange echo carrying over onto his frequency.

He took out his phone and brought up the voice-recording app that he used to remind himself of everything from his grocery list to work projects. Standing at the top of the stairs, he held the phone out, hoping to record the strange voice that was still speaking from somewhere. He couldn't tell which room it was coming from, or even which direction. The voice just seemed all around him, a constant stream of inaudible words.

The voice eventually faded out as Frank slowly moved around, holding his phone out. Once again, the house was deathly quiet. Unnerved, Frank began to head back to the staircase. Just as he reached the top of the stairs, the silence was shattered by the sound of breaking glass. Sharp and clear, it echoed through the house, and Frank swore out loud. This was followed by another sound of glass breaking.

"Forget this," Frank said out loud to himself and rapidly descended the staircase. He raced to the front door and dashed outside and across the perfectly kept yard. As he reached his truck, he glanced back at the house. On the second story, a figure peered out from one of the upstairs windows. It looked like a woman, but when Frank squinted for a better look, she was gone. Frank hopped in his truck.

"Frank, I don't hear a damn thing," said Sam, as he listened to the recording on the phone. "No mumblin' voices, no glass breaking, nothing."

Frank looked at his phone and shook his head in disbelief. "I'm telling ya, I heard what I heard. No idea why it didn't record."

At that moment, the sound of a single gunshot played over the phone's tiny speaker. Sam and Frank both jumped. This was followed by the sound of Frank swearing and racing down the steps.

"What the...." Frank said in disbelief. "Now that I didn't hear!"

Sam stared at the phone as the recording ended with the sound of the company truck starting. He was a practical man who didn't believe in ghosts or anything of that nature. But, growing up in Meridian, he'd heard the stories associated with the Merrehope house and some of the past residents who apparently still resided there.

"Frank, I know you're still new to the area, so I doubt you ever heard any of the stories about the

Merrehope house. Supposedly it's haunted by the daughter of the guy who built it. Eugenia was her name, if my memory serves me well. That could explain the female figure you saw when you were leaving. Most folks who've seen her say she's never any trouble. She's just . . . there."

"And the breaking glass and the gunshot?" asked Frank. "What the hell was that about? That sounded like trouble to me. She's no trouble, my foot."

"Well," Sam said, as he leaned back in his chair. "That one is a little darker. In the 1930s, the house was converted into a boarding house. One of the residents was a school teacher who had some issues. Namely, gambling and booze. Those kinds of issues. I mean, from what I've heard, he was pretty bad off. Toward the end, he was so deep in gambling debts and liquor, folks said he'd just stay in his room talking to himself and wouldn't leave."

Frank leaned forward. "What do you mean by 'toward the end?'"

"One night, in a drunken fit, he lined the mantel of his room with empty whiskey bottles and shot 'em. One by one. Pow! Pow! Pow! Shattered them all. And when there were no more bottles to shoot, well, he put the gun in his mouth and blew his brains out."

Frank's face went white. He looked down at his phone with its recording of a man's final act of self-destruction, sitting ominously on Sam's desk. He stared at it for a bit and then looked back at Sam.

"Why don't you take the rest of the week off, Frank?" Sam finally suggested.

Frank didn't argue.

Stuckey's Bridge
Meridian, Mississippi

Wayne's granddaddy had told him many things. He used to tell him that the area around Stuckey's Bridge in Meridian was haunted, and that he'd best not go down there at night. If you poked around down there, something was bound to poke back. But Wayne never listened to his granddaddy. Not listening to his granddaddy is how Wayne ended up with a three-year sentence at Parchman Farm a few years back. It's also how he ended up standing on the banks of the Chunky River near Stuckey's Bridge in the middle of the night.

He'd been setting out fishing jugs—carefully tying a line and baited hook to an empty milk jug and then placing it out in the water. He planned to come back the next day to see if he'd managed to catch anything. After putting all his jugs out, Wayne was sitting on the bank when he saw a strange light moving across the opposite bank. It silently floated among the trees and gave off a pale-green glow. In the darkness, he could make out nothing else. Every now and then, it would stop, pause for a bit, and then continue moving.

Wayne started to wade out a bit to see if he could get a better look at the light, as it seemed to float up and down the muddy bank. Getting close to the river's edge, he froze. As his granddaddy had told it, the banks of the Chunky River were full of dead folks. All of them butchered by Old Man Stuckey and buried on top of each other like cordwood many years ago.

Boy, if you go in that water, a moldy, rotten hand covered in every foul thing from the bottom of this river is going to silently rise up like a water moccasin. It's going to wrap its dead, wet fingers around your ankle and pull you under. And it will hold you there until your lungs are full of silt and water.

Everybody in Meridian knew the story of Old Man Stuckey. Wayne's granddaddy used to tell stories about the murderous innkeeper who lived on the river and how he would kill and rob his guests. To cover up his crimes, Old Man Stuckey would take the bloody bodies down to the river and either sink them in the muck or bury them in the banks. Wayne couldn't remember what happened to Old Man Stuckey, only that his ghost supposedly still walked the banks of the Chunky River with a lantern in his hand.

The light on the opposite bank moved closer to the water and stopped at its edge. Wayne watched in silence as the eerie light slowly lowered to ground level and stayed there. Peering into the darkness, Wayne could make out a shadowy figure on the opposite shore. As he watched the light slowly descend to the ground, Wayne could've sworn the temperature dropped. Fragments of the stories his granddaddy had told him slinked their way back into his mind.

Some folks say he's still out there, boy. They never did find all the money he got a'killin' all those folks. Some of the bodies were found. Not all of 'em. So there's bodies still out there, probably some money of some sort. And maybe even him.

"A'ight Wayne," he whispered to himself with a chuckle. "Calm down."

Still, that light, he thought. *That ain't no flashlight. Ain't no beam and it ain't . . . shining nowhere.*

A loud thump from the opposite side of the riverbank broke the silence. Unseen night critters jumped into the water, as startled by the noise as Wayne was. The shadowy figure was kneeling next to the light now, but Wayne still couldn't make out who or what it was. The river was deathly quiet, until a low moan broke the silence.

Oh, he'd stab most of 'em, I suppose. That'd be the quickest and easiest way.

The same moan, somewhat weaker than before, sounded out again. No words. Just the moan you make when you're too hurt to form words. The figure on the bank rose up and then stood very still. Wayne's breathing quickened, and he noticed that he could see his breath. While he'd been transfixed on the shadowy figure, the temperature had dropped more.

But they's also some he clubbed to death, according to the old folks. Bashed their heads in and rolled 'em into a hole on the bank.

The next feeble moan was cut short by a loud, hollow-sounding thud, like someone hitting a bag of wet clothes with a large object. The dull thump was repeated a few more times. Each hit was punctuated with a yelp or a moan until there was only silence.

That was enough for Wayne. He bolted from the spot and ran toward his truck that was parked on the dirt road that led to Stuckey's Bridge. Glancing back over his shoulder, he saw the light jerk up from the ground and wave back and forth. The terror of what he'd just witnessed caused his heart to thump in his chest like it was trying to get out. Turning back, he gazed up at the bridge as he navigated the narrow path to the road. It was then that he remembered what his grandfather had told him about Old Man Stuckey's fate.

Course the townsfolk eventually caught him. Can't be carrying on like that and expect not to get caught. They did things different back in the old days. Weren't no trial or nothin'. They convicted him on the spot and hung him from the bridge.

Wayne stopped in his tracks. In the moonlight, he could make out a figure hanging beneath the bridge. Its neck was bent at an impossible angle. Like someone had stretched some taffy. The body silently spun in the nighttime air. Wayne didn't know if he screamed first and then started running or ran as he screamed. He was still screaming when he reached his truck.

Wayne never went out on the Chunky River again. He wouldn't go during daylight hours, and he certainly wouldn't go at night. After all, there were things out on that river and in the woods surrounding it. And dead bodies buried in the mud. When his friends asked him if he wanted to go fishing, he would politely decline their offer. If they pressed the issue, he would tell them why and try to warn them.

Just like his grandfather had tried to warn him.

Cinemark Theater at The Mall at Barnes Crossing
Tupelo, Mississippi

When the movie ended, 13-year-old Mark Bridges stood up from his seat, stretched, and made his way out of the theater in Tupelo. The movie had been OK for a horror flick, but it just wasn't scary enough. Mark couldn't wait until he could go see R-rated horror movies. Everyone said that R-rated horror movies were better. And based on what he had seen late at night on HBO, Mark tended to agree with them.

The bright lights of the lobby caused Mark to squint as he made his way to the arcade. It would still be another 20 minutes or so before the movie that Mark's mother had opted to see would let out, so he had some time to kill. His mother hated horror movies and decided to see some boring historical romance instead. She tricked him into seeing one of those with her a while back by saying it was a war movie. In reality, there had only been about 20 minutes of action in the entire film. The rest of the movie was, as Mark would call it, "boring gushy stuff," with people kissing and whispering how much they loved each other.

The arcade was alive with flashing lights and electronic beeps and boops when he entered. Amazingly enough, it was completely empty, so he wouldn't have to wait behind other people as they finished their games. Although there were several good games here, it was *Street Fighter II* that interested Mark the most. He popped a quarter in, chose Ryu as his character, and immediately entered combat against a hulking brute known as Blanka.

In a flurry of button mashing, Mark easily dispatched Blanka and moved on to his next opponent. He carefully studied the world map and tried to decide who would be his next punching bag. Just as he chose Chun-Li, he noticed in the reflection on the screen that someone was standing behind him.

He couldn't make out who it was, and the person said nothing. She didn't even place a quarter on the game to reserve the next play. The figure just stood silently as Mark squared off against Chun-Li and her arsenal of quick-and-deadly moves. He thought about risking a glance over his shoulder, but to take your eyes off the screen in a game like *Street Fighter II*—even for a second—is a sure way to lose a game.

As he played, the figure stood there silently. Whomever the person was, she didn't move, offer any hints, or criticize Mark's video game skills. She just stood there. Mark tried to concentrate on his game.

When he glanced back up, the figure was now over his left shoulder and seemed to be leaning in closer.

Just as Mark was about to perform the intricate joystick-and-button combo to launch his special fireball attack, he felt a hand gently touch his shoulder.

Forgetting the game, he quickly spun around to confront the figure behind him, but, to his shock, there was no one there. The arcade was just as empty as it had been when he first entered. He was certain there had been someone there. While he stood there stunned, he heard his game end, proving his point about never taking your eyes off the game.

Mark walked back out into the lobby, which was empty except for the theater employees and a small group of people who were just exiting a movie. He finally spotted his mother among the other moviegoers. She was dabbing her eyes with a tissue.

Must've been a tearjerker, he thought.

As they were leaving the theater, he tried to explain what happened, but his mother was too wrapped up in the film she'd just seen to pay him any mind.

"That's nice, Mark," replied his mother, as she fumbled in her purse for her keys. His mother opened her purse and peered into it. She nodded absentmindedly as Mark told her of the vanishing figure in the arcade.

"Oh, you must've seen Lola," said one of the theater employees who overheard their conversation. "She sometimes does stuff like that."

"What?" asked Mark. The employee was an older girl who probably attended the local high school. With his mother distracted in her quest to find her keys, Mark pulled away from her and approached the girl. "What were you saying?"

"I said, that was probably Lola. She's harmless, but it can be a little creepy. This theater is haunted, kid," she said with a smile.

"Get out of here," laughed Mark. "Whoever heard of a haunted multiplex?"

"It's true," the girl said, with a laugh of her own. "I admit it sounds a little silly, but plenty of folks have seen her. Usually out of the corner of their eye or something. Or they will have the feeling that someone is standing directly behind them, but, when they turn around, nobody is there. Some folks have even seen her cleaning up out here. The projection room is haunted as well. That one is a little different. He can be kind of scary."

"Any idea who she is?" inquired Mark, his curiosity getting the better of him. She could just be kidding him, but still, he knew what he saw and felt in the arcade.

"Nope. Rumor is, there used to be a massive farm here many years ago before the mall was built. Seriously. You'd never know, but this was all bottomland and pastures before the mall. Maybe she lived here. Heck, maybe she died here. All I know is, you aren't the only one who's seen or felt her. It actually happens quite a bit."

"Found them," Mark's mother said to no one in particular as she pulled her car keys from her purse. "Let's go, Mark. I want to get home before your dad does."

Mark looked back over his shoulder at his mother, then back to the girl. "I gotta go. Um, thanks for the info, though."

"No problem, kid. Take it easy," the girl replied as she walked off toward the concession stand.

Mark followed his mother toward the theater's exit as she enthusiastically talked about the movie she'd just seen. This time, though, it was Mark who wasn't paying attention. With his mind elsewhere, the two walked out of the theater and into the bright summer day.

Witch Dance
Houston, Mississippi

Author's note: *Although the legend and location of Witch Dance are very real, the story that follows is one of my own design. It is my version of stories that my grandmother would tell me when I was a kid about people who set out to look for the witch that haunts that area—and what happens when they manage to find her.*

"**H**ow do I get myself into these things?" muttered Eric under his breath as he trudged through the woods, trying to keep up with Rachel. Rachel turned and shot him a frustrated look. She was one of what the kids in his class called the "weird girls." Unlike other girls who were into dances, securing their place in the school pecking order, and god-awful pop music, Rachel was into comics, punk rock, and anything horror. And Eric knew exactly how he got himself into these things: he was completely in love with her.

"Will you keep up?" Rachel sighed as Eric got closer. "We don't have all day, and I sure as hell don't want to try to find my way out of these woods after the sun goes down."

"Because of the witch?" Eric replied.

"Well, technically, it's sort of the ghost of a witch or witches, but yes. Because of the witch."

With that, the two walked deeper into the woods together.

The area known as Witch Dance had fascinated Rachel for some time. This past summer, she had stumbled upon a TV show about ghost investigations and paranormal research. Sure, it was a little hokey and probably staged, but her interest was piqued. It wasn't long before she was dragging Eric through abandoned buildings and lonely cemeteries in such of various ghosts and haunts. And now she was dragging Eric deeper into the woods off the Natchez Trace Parkway near Houston in search of whatever lurked around the area known as Witch Dance.

A few weeks ago over lunch, Rachel had told Eric all about Witch Dance and how, many years ago, it had been a meeting place for witches to gather and conduct dark rites and to consort with the devil. The black nights would be filled with spell casting, chanting, and feasting. Then, at some point during the celebrations, the witches would dance around their fire. Legend has it that the ground where they danced had become tainted and nothing would grow there. The dead spots on the ground were still there and had been for many years.

President Andrew Jackson even noted them when he was traveling through the area.

But the story that Rachel liked the most about the area was about a criminal and serial killer named Big Harpe and his encounter with the entity that haunted these woods. In the late 1700s, Big Harpe robbed and murdered up and down the Natchez Trace. Once, after coming upon the dead spots on the ground and learning the story behind them, he dared the witches to come after him as he danced in the middle of one of the dead patches. Shortly after that, he was captured by a posse and beheaded. His severed head was placed on display as a warning to all who sought to emulate his bloody deeds. Later, a woman—rumored to be one of the witches—stole his rotting head. She boiled it, and, once the skull was free of any decaying flesh, she ground it into a powder to make an elixir for her ailing son.

"OK, so it's a bare patch of earth. Wanna go investigate my yard next? I've got a few of those." Eric said. He looked at the patch of barren earth in front of him. The dirt seemed darker than the surrounding ground and, just as the legend said, nothing was growing on this patch. Still, Eric wasn't impressed.

"Will you stop?" Rachel replied, as she snapped a few pictures of the bare areas on her smartphone. "We'll head back soon enough. I just want to look around some more."

"This sucks. At least the other places were interesting. This is just...woods." He looked around at the mass of trees and bramble. "You know I hate the outdoors."

Rachel knelt to get a better look at the bare patch of dark dirt in front of her. "It's completely dead. Just like the stories say. Plenty of grass and plants in other spots."

"It's dead because that's how nature works. Just like my yard. And just like here." With that, Eric stepped onto the desolate patch that Rachel was studying. Rachel looked up. "I mean, this is like a park. I bet folks even have picnics here. There's nothing here."

"I wish you hadn't done that, Eric." Rachel said sternly.

And that's when the clacking sound started.

It started softly. Soft enough that you'd have to pause and listen to make sure you really heard something. Every few seconds, another sharp noise would break the silence. The noise grew somewhat louder and seemed to surround them, like a pack of animals emerging from the deep woods. At times, they could pinpoint the location. At others, the sound would seem to be all around them.

"Rachel, what the hell is that?" Eric asked as he looked around.

"Let's go," Rachel said with an excited smile. With that, she left the trail that led back to their car and began walking deeper into the woods. In their previous excursions into supposedly haunted locations, anytime she heard a strange noise from an attic or another room, Rachel would shoot Eric the same look and dash off in search of its source.

"I hate nature," Eric mumbled and nervously began to follow her as she disappeared deeper into the woods.

For several minutes, they pushed their way through the thick forest toward the mysterious sound that now seemed to be coming from one direction ahead of them. Eric cursed as he walked into yet another thorn bush (the fourth). Pulling the vines off his legs, he continued to walk after Rachel. However, now there was no excitement in Rachel's gait. She walked deliberately and was strangely quiet.

"There's not even a trail here. Couldn't we . . ."

"There's a trail here," interrupted Rachel. Her voice had changed. Gone was the excitement from earlier. Now her voice was flat. Emotionless.

Eric looked down and, strangely enough, there was a trail. Where there had once been just a thick blanket of thorny vines and underbrush, there was now a faint footpath. Sure, it was kind of difficult to spot, but it was there. Still, Eric could've sworn it wasn't there before. He had the stickers embedded into his jeans to prove it.

"Rach," Eric said, looking up. He was going to tell her they probably needed to head back. That it seemed to be getting darker earlier than usual. That he had a general feeling of unease that kept growing with each step he took. That he was starting to feel a little disoriented and that his thinking was getting more and more confused. Like his thought process was working in slow motion.

But when he looked up, Rachel was gone. And the clacking—which had fallen silent—started again.

Eric pressed on for a few more minutes. His unease had given way to the first pangs of real fear. As he looked around, he could swear it was getting darker, even though it was midafternoon. The woods had taken on the grayish shade you see at sunset on an overcast fall day. His grandfather would've called it the gloaming. Rachel was still nowhere to be seen and wasn't responding to his calls. And the clacking sound continued.

He pulled out his iPhone to check the time. He stared at the screen, trying to remember which button to hit to wake it. For a moment he actually couldn't remember how to work his phone. He knew all about his iPhone. How it worked, how to fix it when it wouldn't work, and now he couldn't remember how to wake it. It was a lifeless black thing in his hand. When he finally managed to get the phone to turn on, only his background picture came up. Nothing else loaded on it. No time, no date, no signal bars, nothing. Just his background picture of the smiley face with a drop of blood on it from Alan Moore's comic *Watchmen*.

"OK, we've got to get out of here," he said. "Rachel!" he called out. There was only the sound of his own voice, followed by a faint echo. The woods were completely quiet and still. The only thing Eric could hear was his own uneven breathing. Even the clacking sound had stopped.

Just as he was about to call out for Rachel again, her voice broke the silence. Her voice—like earlier—was flat and emotionless. As best he could tell, it came from behind a small ridge up ahead.

"Eric. Come here. You have to see this."

Pocketing his phone, Eric walked toward the ridge.

By the time he'd crossed it, the sun had set even further and the woods were full of shadows. Rachel was standing at the bottom of the ridge a few feet away from him. She had her back to him and was completely motionless. As Eric approached her, he kept having brief dizzy spells, like he was crossing and uncrossing his eyes. His feet crunched through a thick carpet of dead leaves as he walked toward her. The tiny portion of his brain that was still thinking clearly wondered why there was such a thick layer of dead leaves in the middle of summer.

"Dammit, Rachel," he huffed. "Why didn't you answer me? We're getting the hell out of here. Something is going on, and it's got me freaked out. I feel like I've been drugged or something."

Rachel simply stared ahead with her back to Eric and didn't say a word. Finally, she spoke.

"We finally found something, Eric," she said in that flat, hollow voice. Her voice was even deeper than usual.

More like something found us, said a voice inside Eric's head. He approached her, placed his hands on her shoulders, and spun her around. She pivoted easily, and there was no resistance when he turned her around to face him. Eric backed away in horror.

Rachel's eyes were gone. In their place were two black empty sockets. They looked almost like ink smears. Rachel's mouth was agape, and the front of her hoodie was damp. She'd been drooling.

Over her shoulder, Eric noticed the slumped-over figure emerging from the woods. It was slowly shuffling over toward Rachel and Eric. As far as he could tell, it was an old woman. Matted hair covered her wrinkled, filthy face, and her mouth was filled with blackened gums and a few rotted, yellow teeth. Her clothes were a mass of dirty, mud-streaked rags stitched together. In one withered hand was a stone bowl and in the other a pestle of some sort. She ground the pestle onto the contents of the bowl. Something broke inside the bowl and produced the sharp clacking sound they'd heard earlier.

After boiling the skull, she ground it up in a bowl to use in a potion for her ailing son, Eric remembered Rachel telling him.

As the hideous old crone shuffled closer, Eric tried to run. When he found he was unable to move, he did the next best thing. He started screaming. And soon, he was unable to do even that, and the woods were silent again.

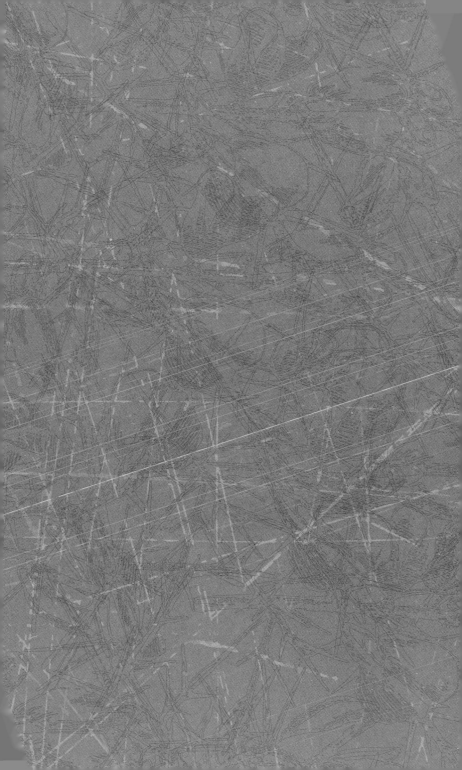

About the Author

Jeff Duke was raised in Tupelo, Mississippi, and began writing at an early age. He formulated a love for all things horror after spending untold hours in detention with books by Stephen King and H.P. Lovecraft. In college, he studied creative writing under Barry Hannah at the University of Mississippi and under Dr. Price Caldwell at Mississippi State University. Although he mainly writes Southern-style "grit lit" these days, he still enjoys writing about horrible things that go bump in the night. Jeff currently resides in Austin, Texas, with his dog, Boone; his cat, Gabbers; and his wife, Angelica, who he still thinks is way out of his league.